This book belongs to:

_____

_____

Written by Jillian Harker
Illustrated by Kristina Stephenson

This is a Parragon Publishing book
First published in 2006

Parragon Publishing
Queen Street House
4 Queen Street
Bath BA1 1HE, UK

ISBN 1-40546-660-X
Printed in China

I Love You, Grandma

Little Bear and Grandma were eating breakfast.

"Grandma," asked Little Bear suddenly, "why do I have such a big nose?"

"To help you find food," Grandma told him.

"But I just looked around and I found these berries," argued Little Bear.

"Ah!" replied Grandma. "Food isn't always that easy to see."

Grandma led Little Bear
down to the river.

"Can you see anything to eat?" she asked.
Little Bear shook his head.
"Can you smell anything?" Grandma added.
"Food," answered Little Bear.
"Then use your nose to find it,"
Grandma told him.

Little Bear followed his nose to some stones on the riverbank. He turned one over.

"A fish!" he laughed.

"Yummy!"

"Dinner," smiled Grandma. "Good job, Little Bear!"
"I love you, Grandma," Little Bear whispered in her ear.

"Grandma," asked Little Bear suddenly, "why do I have such sharp claws?"

"To help you find food," came the reply.

"But you told me I have my nose for that," said Little Bear, surprised.

"Ah!" said Grandma. "Sometimes your nose leads you to food, but you still have to work to get it."

She took Little Bear to the woods.
"Sniff the air!" she reminded him.
Little Bear started to follow his nose.
He stopped at a fallen tree.

"I can smell food," Little Bear said.
"I still can't see it, but I know it's here."
"You'll need to use your claws,"
Grandma told him.

Little Bear dug his sharp claws into the bark. He brok[e]
off a small piece.

"Ants!" he laughed. "Delicious!"

"Lunch," smiled Grandma. "Good work, Little Bear!"

"I love you, Grandma!"

Little Bear yelled.

"Grandma," asked Little Bear suddenly, "why do I have such a long tongue?"

"To help you find food," Grandma said at once.

"But you told me that I have my nose and claws to do that," said Little Bear, surprised.

"Sometimes the best food is hard to reach," Grandma told him.

She took Little Bear to a clearing.
"Smell the air," Grandma said.
Little Bear sniffed hard. He lifted his nose.

"Food!" he told Grandma.
A huge bees' nest hung
from a branch above him.

"I know what to do," laughed Little Bear.

"Look at me!"

he called.

He hooked the nest with his sharp claws,
lifted it down, and opened it up.

"Honey!" he smiled. "Mmmmm!"

"Supper," said Grandma. But Little Bear's big
claws couldn't reach the food.

"So what are you going to do now?" asked Grandma.
"Use my long tongue," laughed Little Bear.

And that's just what he did.
"Brilliant, Little Bear!" laughed Grandma.

"How do you know so many things, Grandma?" asked Little Bear suddenly.

"That's easy," Grandma smiled. "When I was small, I was curious ... just like you," she said. "You ask so many questions, you'll soon know lots of things, too."

And she hugged Little Bear tight.

"Do you know I love you, Grandma?"
asked Little Bear.
"I do!" answered Grandma.
She stroked Little Bear's sticky head.

"And you know I love you, too," she said.